# The Big Woolly Jumper

A humorous story
in a familiar setting

First published in 2005 by
Franklin Watts
96 Leonard Street
London
EC2A 4XD

Franklin Watts Australia
45–51 Huntley Street
Alexandria
NSW 2015

Text © Damian Harvey 2005
Illustration © Mike Spoor 2005

The rights of Damian Harvey to be identified as the author
and Mike Spoor as the illustrator of this Work have
been asserted in accordance with the Copyright, Designs
and Patents Act, 1988.

A CIP catalogue record for this book is available
from the British Library.

ISBN 0 7496 5942 4 (hbk)
ISBN 0 7496 5948 3 (pbk)

**Series Editor:** Jackie Hamley
**Series Advisors:** Dr Barrie Wade, Dr Hilary Minns
**Design:** Peter Scoulding


Printed in Hong Kong / China

# The
# Big Woolly
# Jumper

Written by
## Damian Harvey

Illustrated by
## Mike Spoor

# FRANKLIN WATTS
### LONDON•SYDNEY

## Damian Harvey

"When I was little, my gran gave me big woolly jumpers. I had to wear them every time she came to visit. Yuck!"

## Mike Spoor

"When I was little, my mum made me a knitted swimming costume! I didn't like it very much, as you can see!"

Grandma had knitted a great
big woolly jumper.

She wrapped it up and sent it
to William for his birthday.

6

But it hung past his knees ...

... it covered his ears ...

... and it made him itch.

"Yuck!" said William.

"Can I take it off now?"

11

"Not yet!" said Mum. "Go and
say thank you to Grandma first.

"You can take Max with you."

William tried to put Max's lead on, but Max would not sit still.

15

"Stop!" shouted William.

But Max did not stop.

William chased Max
down the street ...

... and around the corner.

William chased Max *all* round
the park ...

... and *all* the way up the lane
to Grandma's house.

The great big woolly jumper
got smaller and smaller and smaller.

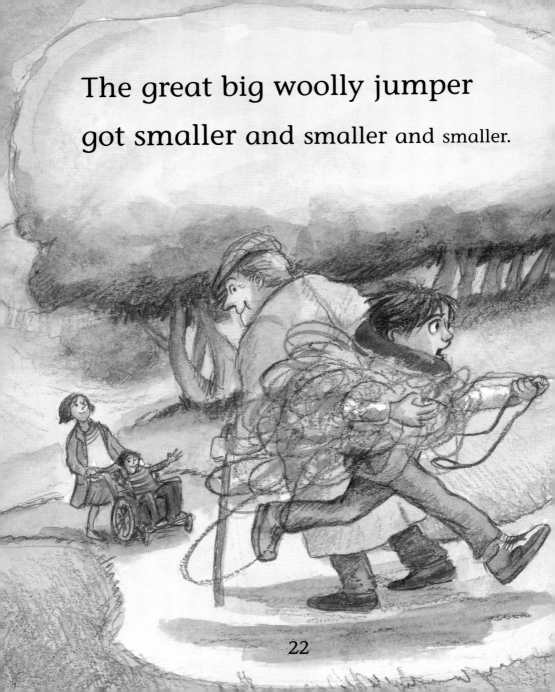

23

24

In the end, all that was left
was a great big pile of wool.

"Thank you," said Grandma.

"That's just what I need."

27

The next day, Grandma brought *another* present for William.

"They will go with your big
woolly jumper!" said Grandma.

# Notes for parents and teachers

**READING CORNER** has been structured to provide maximum support for new readers. The stories may be used by adults for sharing with young children. Primarily, however, the stories are designed for newly independent readers, whether they are reading these books in bed at night, or in the reading corner at school or in the library.

Starting to read alone can be a daunting prospect. **READING CORNER** helps by providing visual support and repeating words and phrases, while making reading enjoyable. These books will develop confidence in the new reader, and encourage a love of reading that will last a lifetime!

If you are reading this book with a child, here are a few tips:

**1.** Make reading fun! Choose a time to read when you and the child are relaxed and have time to share the story.

**2.** Encourage children to reread the story, and to retell the story in their own words, using the illustrations to remind them what has happened.

**3.** Give praise! Remember that small mistakes need not always be corrected.

**READING CORNER** covers three grades of early reading ability, with three levels at each grade. Each level has a certain number of words per story, indicated by the number of bars on the spine of the book, to allow you to choose the right book for a young reader:

| **GRADE 1** | **GRADE 2** | **GRADE 3** |
|---|---|---|
| 50 words | 130 words | 250 words |
| 70 words | 160 words | 350 words |
| 100 words | 200 words | 450 words |